The Land Beyond
the Setting Sun

The Land Beyond the Setting Sun

THE STORY OF SACAGAWEA

By Tracy M. Leininger

Layout and Design by Joshua Goforth and Noelle Wheeler
Illustrations by Kelly Pulley and Lisa Reed
Production Coordinator Cathy Craven

Printed in the United States of America by Jostens Commercial Publications
ISBN 1-929241-19-4

HIS SEASONS™

8122 Datapoint Drive
Suite 900
San Antonio, TX 78229
(210) 490-2101
www.hisseasons.com

To Kelly Welch, my dear sister and best friend. It is Kelly's example of courage and strength in the Lord that inspired me to pen the thoughts in this story.

Also, to my dear friends who have tirelessly encouraged and supported me throughout this exciting adventure.

The heavens declare the glory of God;

And the firmament shows His handiwork.

Psalm 19:1

CHAPTER ONE

The God of Creation

Many years ago, when the western plains were still a vast unexplored mystery to the people of the newly formed United States, there lived a young Shoshone Indian girl named Sacagawea. Like her ancestors before her, Sacagawea grew up in the shadows of the great Rocky Mountains.

Her people were not the strongest or richest of tribes, but they lived a contented life. In fact, the Shoshone were known to be the most fun-loving and cheerful in all the land. Their laws emphasized honesty and generosity, and they gladly shared what little they possessed. But, the most highly esteemed virtue was bravery. Those who possessed this trait gained the greatest honor and respect.

The warriors often indulged in their favorite pastime—telling stories of heroic deeds to eager listeners. Sacagawea, who loved to hear these tales, often stood quietly by the campfire and listened with intense fascination as the strong warriors recounted their rigorous journeys beyond the mountains in the land of the setting sun. Sacagawea was small for a ten-year-old, but her courageous heart gave her strength. Even though the tall braves shadowed her tanned face from the firelight, her deep brown eyes glistened with the light of adventure that burned within.

Sacagawea could hardly contain her excitement as the warriors described "Great Waters" sparkling in the sunshine as far as the eye could see. The braves claimed these waters contained so many fish that they had to swim up the rivers and streams to make room for others. Sacagawea could scarcely imagine such abundant game. To her, this land beyond the setting sun held the promise of rich discoveries, great adventure, and endless beauty. She hoped that some day she might be able to see for herself what now she could only imagine—the "Great Waters" in the land beyond the mountains.

At times, Sacagawea heard the warriors describe battles against their enemies. The greatest enemy of the Shoshone was the Minnetare* tribe from the land of the Great Plains, in the direction of the rising sun. Hearing of the large herds of grazing buffalo and lush vegetation, Sacagawea believed this land to be full of wonderful things. But she never desired to go there, for the braves told of the harsh ways of the Minnetare warriors.

One evening, Sacagawea heard a Shoshone brave report the startling news that the cruel Minnetare had taken captives from a neighboring tribe. "How sad to be taken from your people," Sacagawea thought to herself. A sick feeling filled her stomach as she looked around her little village. "What would I do if I never again saw my mountain homeland and my family?" Sacagawea shuddered as she thought of the poor captives, but she was not afraid. She felt secure sitting among the braves of her tribe.

Sacagawea feared very little. Even at a young age she was noted for her bravery—the trait her tribe esteemed more than any other. She possessed the natural ability to make sensible decisions in the face of extreme danger.

*Minnetare—also known as the Hidasta

Sacagawea found enjoyment in life, even in her small, daily tasks. Picking berries and drying them for food was one of the many duties of the Indian women and children. Sacagawea loved this task because it gave her a chance to enjoy nature. Many times, she would search farther and longer than any of the other women, imagining she was exploring the land beyond the mountains. She would close her eyes and dream of "Great Waters" that danced in the sunlight, and where fish were so abundant that they played in the streams.

On one such day, Sacagawea searched even farther than usual, and came upon a meadow she had never seen before. Entering the clearing, Sacagawea paused, her sharp eyes scanning the tree line. Though brave, Sacagawea had been trained as a young girl to understand the dangers of life in the mountains. But she was drawn to explore the delights of creation, in spite of the dangers that might await her.

The sweet fragrance of primroses and poppies filled the fresh air. The summer sun had so cheered the surrounding world that everything in it seemed to come alive in new and captivating ways. Bumblebees buzzed about the flowers and birds joined in jubilant song as they flitted among the chokeberry bushes that thrived along mountain spring waters.

Caught up in the loveliness around her, Sacagawea forgot all about picking berries, forgot all about her tribe below, and for a time, even forgot about the land beyond the mountains. The beauty of nature enthralled her, and her heart sang along with the meadowlarks. She busied herself picking wildflowers and braiding them into her long black hair.

After enjoying the discoveries of the meadow, she lay down in its soft, green grass and looked up at the spacious sky. She watched the clouds drift by in the soft breeze, and wondered, "Who is the Great Creator who made all these things for me to enjoy? We have a sun god, a moon god, a god of the harvest, and a god of rain, but who is the God over all? Who makes the birds each sing their own song? Who tells the geese to fly away before the winter snow? Who made the antelope and gave him such speed?"

Sacagawea's mind filled with more and more questions. She realized that whoever this God of creation was, He must be powerful. The more she looked at nature around her, in all its order and diversity, the more she marveled at the greatness of this unknown creator, this God of all gods. After some time, Sacagawea became tired from pondering all her unanswered questions and fell into a dreamy sleep.

The earth is the LORD's, and all its fullness,

the world and those who dwell therein.

Psalm 24:1

CHAPTER TWO

The Thrilling Chase

The neigh of a horse suddenly awakened Sacagawea. Where was she? And who sat upon the horse towering over her? At first her cloudy mind refused to clear, then suddenly everything came back. Sacagawea jumped to her feet and looked up into the eyes of her brother, Cameahwait. He was ten years older, and though they were good friends, he was like a father to her, watching after and protecting her.

"Sacagawea," he cautioned, "do you not know the dangers of the mountains? There are bears who would love to find you as I have just now." Reaching down, Cameahwait took her hand and swung her up onto his horse. With a twinkle in his eye, and changing his tone of voice he said, "Come. If you wish to explore this mountain range, you must

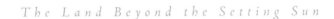
stay with me. We are hunting antelope. Soon the game will come this way, and it will be my turn to take the chase."

The Shoshone Indians did not have guns, and to kill an antelope with bow and arrow, a brave must first wear the animal down by chasing it and making it run a great distance. Five to six braves, mounted on horseback, would station themselves at strategic points across the mountain range, then take turns chasing the animal.

It was not the custom for an Indian brave to bring a girl on such a hunt, but Cameahwait knew of Sacagawea's love of adventure and admired her courageous spirit. He esteemed her more than any of the women in their tribe, though she was still a girl.

Suddenly, just as her brother promised, an antelope burst into the far end of the meadow, followed closely by a brave riding a horse that bore marks of great fatigue.

"Wrap your legs around the horse's side and keep your arms tight around my waist," Cameahwait instructed, as he dug his heels into the side of the stallion. The

horse's eyes glowed with spirit, as he lurched into a swift gallop across the meadow. They disappeared into the forest with Cameahwait and Sacagawea letting out whoops of exhilaration.

The wind tore through Sacagawea's hair as they rode, ripping out all the flowers. Sacagawea did not even notice, for all her attention was focused on clinging to the bare back of the stallion and dodging overhanging branches. The thrill of the chase made her heart pound as she and her brother covered ground that Sacagawea had never seen before. Over ridges, down steep inclines, and through endless meadows they pursued the swift antelope that bounded before them.

When at last their horse displayed fatigue, another brave took their place. The chase continued without them, and Cameahwait turned their horse homeward. Sacagawea looked at her brother and exclaimed with a bright smile, "I think I am the happiest girl that has ever lived." The peaceful meadow, the thrilling ride, and the companionship of her brother—who planned this day for her enjoyment? Again she

wondered, "Who created all things, and who is the God of all gods?" Her people did not know, or else they would have told her. Sacagawea did not know where to find the answer to her questions, but she knew she *must* find out.

But as for you, you meant evil against me; but

God meant it for good, in order to bring it about

as it is this day, to save many people alive.

Genesis 50:20

CHAPTER THREE

Captured

At the end of summer, Sacagawea's tribe moved their camp out of the mountain meadow to live along the banks of the Snake River. This winter location was better for hunting and survival, but it offered the Shoshone less protection from marauding tribes.

Sacagawea and her family were among the first to make the move. The few families that had already camped along the river quickly made preparations for the coming winter. Autumn winds blew, telling of the snow soon to come. The chilly air motivated the men to hunt and fish with fresh determination. They knew that their success or failure meant feast or famine during the long winter months. Sacagawea and the other women spent their time cooking and drying meats as well as preparing furs for trade.

One cool morning, Sacagawea began the tedious process of stretching out a deer hide. Suddenly, she heard whoops and hollers coming from the thicket across the river. Sacagawea's sharp eyes darted up and gazed intently into the thicket.

"Have the men already returned from their hunt?" she wondered aloud. Bursting from the thicket came Cameahwait with three other Shoshone braves, their horses heaving from exhaustion. Sacagawea's delight at seeing her brother soon turned to alarm as she saw Minnetare warriors following closely at their heels. The rest of the Shoshone hunting party had already been attacked and overpowered by the fierce Minnetare. Cameahwait and a few other survivors had escaped and raced back to the camp to warn the women and children of their danger.

"Run! Run for your lives!" shouted Cameahwait. "Our warriors have been ambushed and your only hope is to run!" In desperation, Cameahwait led the pursuing war party to a deeper river crossing, hoping to slow the enemy down.

His plan might have worked, but the swift current proved too powerful, sweeping his horse down the river and out of sight. Seeing his failure to cross, the Minnetare warriors chose a shallower part of the river and quickly forged through. Lunging up the banks, they rushed upon the helpless women and children before they had enough time to find sufficient cover in the nearby woods.

Sacagawea had hidden beneath some thick underbrush, but one warriors sharp eyes soon tracked her path. A strong arm reached down and jerked Sacagawea out of her refuge. The warrior flung her upon his horse and galloped away.

The wild ride that followed did not give Sacagawea the thrill that it had when she rode with her brother. This time, instead of trying to hold on, all her strength was focused on throwing herself off the horse's back. Try as she might, she could not escape. The cruel Minnetare's grip grew steadily tighter around her waist.

"I will not fear," she said to herself. "It is just a matter of time before Cameahwait will track me down and take me back to my people." Hour after hour they rode toward the land of the rising sun, and all that was familiar to Sacagawea faded away. Her heart filled with anxiety over what might be happening to the rest of her family and to her tribe.

Back at the Snake River camp, all was still. Not one Indian remained. Before all was over, the Minnetare warriors killed four men, four women, several boys, and took captive the remaining women and children. In hopes of rescuing the captives, the few surviving Shoshone braves had retreated into the mountains to seek help from the main camp.

Evening fell, and Sacagawea's captor finally halted his horse. They dismounted and entered some thick underbrush. Coming to a clearing, she was surprised to see many Shoshone women and children. They were bound hand and foot, and Sacagawea felt distressed to see their helplessness. Even more disturbing was that neither her mother or sister were among the captives. Her heart sank as she imagined what might have happened to them. She longed for the comfort of her mother and the companionship of her sister.

Bound as the others, Sacagawea hardly slept that night. The reality of being a captive began to sink in. Would she ever see her family again? What about her native homeland—would she ever return? The happy years she had lived among her people, and the fond memories of exploring the high mountain meadows seemed like a far away dream. So much had changed in just one day. Where was the God of creation? Perhaps He could help her.

The Minnetare awakened their captives early and continued on foot. It seemed to Sacagawea that the warriors had chosen the most difficult terrain just to taunt them in their weakened state. Her hands were still bound, and the rawhide cut into her wrists. The captives were forced to follow behind the warrior's horses at a very fast pace. They had not eaten since the day before, and the hunger pains in Sacagawea's stomach were almost unbearable. To her dismay, they journeyed farther and farther from the land beyond the mountains. The foothills of her mountain home disappeared behind miles of rolling hills, lush with waving grasses and full of grazing buffalo.

In spite of her captivity, Sacagawea took pleasure in watching the great buffalo. Cameahwait had told her all about the great herds in the land below. Now she recalled his words with comfort.

"Sacagawea," he had once told her, "there are many lessons that you can learn from the buffalo, but the most important of all is that of courage and determination. You see," he went on, "during the coldest and hardest winter blizzards, the buffalo are never afraid, and they never go into hiding like the great brown bear. No, the buffalo stand firm in the storm and keep their faces to the wind, no matter how fierce it may be." Cameahwait had smiled at his little sister and continued, "You show much courage already for one so young. When you grow older, never forget this lesson: no matter how great the storm in life becomes—always keep your face to the wind."

Sacagawea took a deep breath as she trudged on. "Always keep your face to the wind," she whispered. "That is what I must do, no matter what lies ahead. I must face life with the same dauntless spirit that is so respected among our people."

Ransomed

The years passed, marked by many hardships. Sacagawea served as a slave in the camp of her captors and was treated with little respect. Despite her unpleasant conditions, Sacagawea grew into an attractive young woman. Her dark brown eyes never lost the glimmer of hope and determination that still flickered within her heart.

Sacagawea often thought of the lessons her brother had taught her. Many times when surviving another day seemed almost impossible, she gained strength from watching the sun set against the western sky. As she looked toward her homeland, Sacagawea comforted herself with something her brother had told her when times were difficult. "The skies with the most clouds make the prettiest sunsets."

"If this is true," Sacagawea thought to herself, "then no matter how many clouds this present trial brings, the end will be that much more beautiful." Turning back toward the Minnetare camp, she would often whisper a prayer to the God of creation, asking Him to give her strength and to deliver her from captivity. Though she still did not know His name, she knew that there *must* be a God who had created all things.

One afternoon, during Sacagawea's fourth year of slavery, a French fur trader came to the Minnetare village. This was the first white man Sacagawea had ever seen. She was so intrigued with the strong foreigner that she could not stop looking at him. His sparkling eyes reminded her of the deep, blue-green lakes in her old mountain homeland. While skinning a beaver, she realized the white man was returning her gaze. Blushing, Sacagawea focused intently on the beaver pelt and began to work as fast as she could, not daring to look back up.

"If I were a daughter of the chieftain," thought Sacagawea, "he would make me his squaw, but I am just a slave girl and of little value." Even so, Sacagawea carried herself with an air of grace and confidence that made her look like anything but a slave.

Little did Sacagawea know, but the Frenchman, Touissant Charbonneau, had already taken notice of her. From the beginning, he admired her beauty, the confident way she carried herself, and her determination to work hard. She seemed to take delight in her work, conquering even the most menial tasks without complaint.

One evening, shortly after the white man had come to the Minnetare village, Sacagawea saw him talking with the Chieftain by the campfire. As she walked by, Sacagawea could not help but overhear their words.

"Humph!" grunted the old chieftain. "You want to make Shoshone woman your squaw? I trade squaw for ten beaver pelts and half of your beads and supplies."

This was all that Sacagawea heard as she walked past, their voices mingling with the sounds of the night air. Her heart seemed to stand still for a moment, then raced in nervous anticipation.

"The white fur trader has chosen me to be his wife?" She wondered in disbelief. "Surely there must be some mistake!"

That evening as she lay in her tepee, Sacagawea tossed and turned as anxious thoughts filled her mind. She tried to sleep, but her heart would not rest. One moment she was hopeful, thinking about being freed from her captivity; the next moment she was overcome with uncertainty.

"What if the white man cannot afford to pay my ransom?" Sacagawea worried. She shuddered at the thought of living one more day in the Minnetare village. "But then, what if he *does* take me away, and I am not happy? What if he is not as kind as he appears?" Finally, unable to come to any conclusions, she fell into a fitful sleep.

It was not long before Sacagawea found out that Touissant Charbonneau had indeed fallen in love with her. He not only paid her ransom, but soon after, they were married. They moved near to the Mandan tribe, where they lived peacefully for one year.

Sacagawea learned to love the ways of the white man, and it was with great interest that, in 1804, she welcomed Meriwether Lewis, William Clark, and their expedition to stay the winter in their village. Sacagawea's heart filled with excitement when she learned that the purpose of the expedition was to seek out a passage to the "Great Waters."

"Sacagawea," her husband asked her one evening, "do you remember if your people had many horses?"

"My people were poor, but we took pride in our horses," Sacagawea replied.

"If you were able to travel west with this expedition, could you lead us to your people?" Charbonneau questioned. "Would you remember how to get there?"

Sacagawea's heart leaped. "I could never forget the way to my own people!" she exclaimed. "When do we go?"

"Patience, my little wife. There are many things that must take place before we can leave. Lewis and Clark need an interpreter, and that is why they want me. They also need to be guided to a tribe that can get them horses to help them cross the great mountains. That is why they need you. But winter is coming, and you will soon give birth to our first child." Charbonneau smiled and continued. "I know that if any woman could be strong-hearted enough to make that long journey with a small baby, it would be you, but we must wait and see. If God wills it, then I will not stand in the way of making that journey."

Sacagawea sighed as her thoughts turned to the God of the white man. Her husband had said that this God was the God of all gods, and, that not only did He create all things, He also cares for and loves His people.

There was still so much about this God that Sacagawea did not understand. "Does He care about the child I will soon deliver?" she wondered. "Does He care if I ever see my people again or the land beyond the mountains that I have so often dreamed of?"

Deep in her heart, a ray of light shone forth and filled her with the hope that perhaps God *did* care and that maybe this was the purpose for her capture. Maybe God had planned the past hardships to prepare her for this journey. But for now, she could only wait.

In February of 1805, Sacagawea gave birth to a healthy baby boy whom she and Charbonneau named Jean Baptiste, which is French for John the Baptist.

"We will give him this name," declared his happy father, "because, just like John the Baptist in the Bible, he will prepare a way in the wilderness. God willing, he will one day tell many Indian nations of the Christ who has come."

The God of all gods had given them this healthy child and the strength to join the expedition. Though there were many things she did not know about God, Sacagawea's heart swelled with joy at the thought of telling her people about the Creator, His Son, Jesus, and why she and her husband had named their son after John the Baptist.

The snow was melting off the river banks, making little streams on the icy crust over the water. All too slowly for Sacagawea, the river began to thaw. Soon, even the air that she breathed seemed rich with promise as they made final preparations for their journey.

Everyone shared Sacagawea's excitement on April 7, 1805, when Lewis and Clark packed up their winter camp. With their six canoes and two pirogues,* they were eager to press on to a land where no white man had ever dared to go. The explorers were heading into the great unknown. But to Sacagawea, the only woman on the journey, this land was all she had known from childhood. With two-month-old Jean strapped to her back, Sacagawea started upon the journey without fear or anxious thought of the future. She was not merely a guide for the expedition—she was homeward bound. The challenges and adventures that lay ahead filled her with anticipation and wonder.

pirogues - any boat resembling a canoe in shape

CHAPTER FIVE

Bravery in the Rapids

The first month of the journey moved slowly but steadily, as the explorers grew accustomed to uncharted territory. Sacagawea and her little family became a great asset to the expedition. Not only did all the men admire the brave Indian squaw with the little papoose strapped to her back, but they grew to appreciate her kindness as well. She never complained, and she was always ready to serve the men by making tasty meals with the herbs and wild mushrooms she collected along the way. Charbonneau would, on occasion, surprise them when he prepared wild game with his secret French recipes.

One afternoon, the party was paddling their way up river against the strong current. In the distance, they heard the sound of water crashing and breaking.

"Could it be the great waterfall leading to the first mountain range the Indians had spoken of?" they wondered. With mounting anticipation, they forged up the rushing waters. But this was no waterfall. The current grew swifter, and their hearts filled with dread as they paddled hard against the churning waters. The man in charge of the pirogue's rudder panicked at the sight of the rapids and lost control of the boat. The wind took hold of the sails and turned the little ship on its side, causing the boat to fill with water. Many of the expedition's necessary items and valuables, including medicine, food, journals, and gunpowder, disappeared into the rushing waters. Their very lives were in danger as the boat began to sink into the murky waters.

"Dear God," Charbonneau cried, "please have mercy on us and save us all!"

Hearing her husband, Sacagawea prayed silently, "Dear Creator of all, give me strength, for I know that all things come from you. Without you I can do nothing."

God's peace immediately flooded Sacagawea's heart. With new-found courage,

Sacagawea grabbed a rope to keep from being swept away and jumped into the water with her baby still strapped to her back. She quickly retrieved all that she could reach.

Meanwhile, one of the explorers grabbed his gun and pointed it at the man whose fear and lack of self-control was threatening the lives of everyone. "I'll shoot you if you don't take hold of the rudder and behave like a man!" he yelled.

The man immediately regained his composure, and as soon as the boat was righted, everyone worked diligently to bail water. Sacagawea pulled herself back into the boat along with all the rescued supplies.

Later that evening, after the men set up camp, Clark spoke gratefully to Sacagawea. "You do not know how much we owe you." Then he added with a slight laugh, "You had fortitude equal to any man aboard that boat."

Impressed by the bravery and sacrifice of the young woman, the explorers all agreed that the next river they discovered should be named after her.

Although honored that the men chose to name the river after her, Sacagawea was still overwhelmed with the new peace and joy that she felt in her heart. She now knew that the God of all gods, the Creator of all, was also the God in control of all things. He knew the anxieties and thoughts of her heart, and He cared for and loved her personally. He was her Heavenly Father to whom she could go in troubled times—someone who could speak to her heart and comfort her.

With each passing day, Sacagawea grew more excited. She could hardly wait to see her people and tell them of her God. One day, however, she was gripped with a sudden thought. What if her family did not escape the Minnetare raid that day? Sacagawea could still faintly see the picture of when she last saw her brother, Cameahwait, being swept down the river in the strong current. What if he was not able to get to shore? What if her awful captors had killed him? Shuddering, Sacagawea closed her eyes and silently asked God to give her strength for whatever lay ahead.

For lo, the winter is past, the rain is over and gone.

The flowers appear on the earth;

the time of singing has come. . .

Song of Solomon 2:11-12a

CHAPTER SIX

The Prettiest Sunsets

The expedition continued on its way, passing fertile plains lush with grass and teeming with herds of buffalo and elk. Occasionally they spotted a solitary antelope standing with its regal head held high, surveying its surroundings with a confident, yet alert, air. Down by the riverbanks grew countless yellow and red currants, gooseberries, chokecherries, and an abundance of wild roses, adding to the thriving beauty around them. Now with the month of June in full bloom, the party could see the distant mountains jutting majestically out of the plains and capped by snowy peaks that melted into the skyline.

The scenery did much to boost the spirits of the weary travelers, but many were the trials and unexpected setbacks that came with covering new territory. Once, they were attacked by great grizzly bears who seemed to have nine lives before the men were finally able to kill them. Encounters with fearsome panthers and stampeding buffalo threatened their lives. A rainy season brought with it a flash flood that sent a wall of water rushing down the river, nearly wiping out the entire party. Everyone managed to escape just in time, although the churning waters claimed more of their precious supplies. Sacagawea lost all her possessions, even Jean Baptiste's much-needed carrier.

Though she never complained, Sacagawea's health began to wear down. The ill effects of the cold water capsizing, combined with the strenuous travels, were taking their toll. At first, she ignored the fever and pressed on without telling anyone of her suffering. However, the sharp eye of Lewis, who had some medical experience, took notice of her failing health, and he immediately gave her the appropriate medicine. But Sacagawea had kept her sickness a secret so long that it was almost too advanced to remedy. She grew deathly ill, and when it came time to continue their journey on foot, she had to be carried. Lewis and Clark both feared for her life, and daily grew more concerned.

When coherent, Sacagawea spent much time in prayer with her new-found God, gaining comfort and strength. "God of Creation, I know that You made me, and I know that You are in control of all things. I know that You have directed my steps all the way, even into captivity, so that I might lead these white men to the land beyond the setting sun. I know that You have not led me into this wilderness only to leave me here. Please, give me the strength to carry on and to find my people and tell them of You."

Slowly but surely, she began to regain her strength and returned to health. By the beginning of August, the land and terrain had become familiar to Sacagawea, and she was once again full of spirit. Yet, there was still no sign of her Shoshone people.

"We are very near my people," she assured Lewis and Clark. "We will find their camp within a few days." Sacagawea spoke with confidence, but she felt a pain in her heart as she wondered whether her tribe was truly to be found or if they lived no more.

The expedition came to the very spot where the Minnetare had raided their camp five years before. Sacagawea's heart sank when she saw that there was no sign of tribal life. The memories came flooding back and she closed her eyes trying to forget that awful day. Though she asked God for courage on the inside, she remained perfectly confident on the outside, once again assuring Lewis and Clark that there was no cause for alarm.

"My people move their camp according to the changing seasons and settle where the game is plentiful," she explained. "I feel sure that they are still higher in the mountains. When we find them," she said with native pride, "you will meet good and generous people and strong horses that will take you over these mountains."

Lewis and Clark split up in hopes of finding Sacagawea's tribe, and although one brave was sighted, he retreated so quickly that they were unable to distinguish which tribe he was from.

Sacagawea's prayers became more frequent until late one evening, when a messenger arrived from Lewis' men. He said they had found a tribe fitting the description of her people. But they needed Sacagawea before they could be sure.

"Be still my heart," Sacagawea whispered to herself as tears of joy mixed with anxiety sprang into her eyes. "I must wait until the morning light to see if these are my people and if my family still lives."

The next morning, Sacagawea awoke as the first light appeared on the eastern horizon. The stars in the sky above still quietly twinkled—a blissful reminder to Sacagawea that she was finally home. As the soft wind stirred through the pines, it carried with it the song of a lone elk's bugle. The cool dew on the grass sent shivers up her spine as she stretched and gazed about the sleeping camp.

Sacagawea knew she was indeed home at last. A flood of memories swept over her, and she could scarcely wait to see if her people still lived. The place where Lewis and his men planned to meet them lay just over the next ridge. It was all Sacagawea could do to keep from going ahead of the rest. To her great relief, she did not have to wait long, for the others soon roused themselves and packed up camp.

Cresting the ridge, Sacagawea looked into the meadow below and could faintly make out the native dress of her people in the dawn's light. A cry of delight escaped her lips as she rushed ahead of the group, tearing down the mountainside with tears of joy streaming down her cheeks. As she broke through the trees surrounding the meadow, she nearly ran into a warrior, decorated in the highest honor of chieftain.

Sacagawea looked up into his eyes and saw that she was face-to-face with her brother, Cameahwait! Both stood for a moment in complete shock. Then Sacagawea found herself sobbing for joy in his strong embrace. Although Cameahwait was a stoic chieftain, those witnessing the scene were almost sure they saw tears in his eyes as well.

That night, Sacagawea watched the sun sink behind the great mountains of her homeland. As the rays cast their light on the clouds, Charbonneau said that it seemed as if the Master Artist Himself, was painting a glorious masterpiece on His heavenly canvas.

Sacagawea whispered to herself, "The God of creation led me to the land of the rising sun and into slavery. But then, in the midst of the clouds, He gave me Charbonneau, little Jean Baptiste, and best of all, a knowledge of Himself, the God of all gods. Now He has allowed me to see my people, and I can tell them of the God of creation before we continue our journey to the land beyond the mountains."

Behind her lay blessings amidst the trials. Ahead lay the land of wonders that she had dreamed of for so long—the land with the "Great Waters" that dance in the sunshine and fish so abundant that they jump and play in the starlight.

Sacagawea's heart was filled with gratitude and contentment. "Yes," she sighed, "Cameahwait is right—the cloudiest skies *do* make the prettiest sunsets."

To give them beauty for ashes, the oil of joy for mourning,

the garment of praise for the spirit of heaviness;

that they may be called trees of righteousness,

the planting of the LORD, that He may be glorified.

Isaiah 61:3

Conclusion

Sadly, Sacagawea learned that her brother Cameahwait and her sister's son were the only members of her family who survived the Minnetare raid. Though it was hard for Sacagawea to leave her native tribe, her heart was now with her husband, and the thought of traveling with the expedition to the land beyond the mountains gave her renewed determination.

Lewis and Clark's expedition sighted the "Great Waters," known as the Pacific Ocean, on November 7, 1805. They were the first white men to travel completely across the United States.

By August 14, 1806, the expedition had returned to the Mandan village. There they sadly bid farewell to Sacagawea, Charbonneau, and eighteen-month-old Jean Baptiste. The rigors of the journey had bonded the group together with a tie that would never be broken. Clark especially took a liking to Sacagawea's little son and offered to pay for his education back east.

Their parting did not last long. Within a year, Charbonneau decided to accept a job offer from Clark and moved his family into a log cabin in the little town of St. Louis, Missouri. Keeping his word, Clark paid Jean's way through school from the time he was six years old. During his years at the university, Jean met a prince from Germany who was intrigued with his Indian heritage and offered to take him to Germany. Grateful for the opportunity, Jean Baptiste accepted, and left the shores of his homeland.

While in Germany, Jean studied diligently, learning many languages, but, as time passed, his Native American blood stirred within him, and he knew that he must return to the heart of his homeland.

Jean Baptiste not only returned to America, but to his original people, the Shoshone, in their picturesque mountain homeland. Like his father, he became a trapper, interpreter, and fur trader, and lived with his mother's people until his death.

He has made everything beautiful in its time.

Also He has put eternity in their hearts . . .

Ecclesiastes 3:11a

Author's Notes

I absolutely love history, and find it exciting to see the hand of God guiding human events to accomplish His providential plan. While researching the Lewis and Clark Expedition, prior to writing *The Land Beyond the Setting Sun,* it amazed me to see God's clear design for Sacagawea's life. Even in her most challenging times, He was preparing her for *His* purposes. It was through her captivity that she was ultimately delivered and able to help guide the first white men across the plains of America.

As a Christian, it encourages me to know that God makes "beauty from ashes and joy from gloom." When trying times come in your life, dear reader, you can face them with the confidence that He *does* make all things beautiful in His time.

The significance of Sacagawea's son's name, John the Baptist, is profound because at that time in history, the light of Christ had not yet been proclaimed to the western half of the United States. Lewis and Clark's expedition was the key that unlocked that wilderness. As the first John the Baptist, who prepared the way for Christ in the wilderness, Sacagawea's little son played a role in opening up the Northwest Territory so the light of Christ could penetrate this uncharted land.